MW01045117

Robin with the Red Hat

Sukhdev Kaur Dosanjh

VANTAGE PRESS
New York

FIRST EDITION

Published by Vantage Press, Inc.
516 West 34th Street, New York, New York 10001

Manufactured in the United States of America
ISBN: 0-533-12227-9

0 9 8 7 6 5 4 3 2 1

To my three children, who demanded
that I publish my children's books;
And to Herman, my son presently
completing his law degree;
Aneep, my daughter presently
completing her university degree;
Amanbir, my son presently in high
school.

And to my father, S. Pakhar Singh
Dosanjh, who admired and
encouraged my writing.

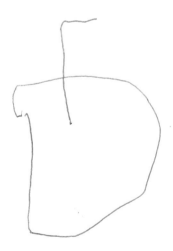

It was springtime, when mountains seemed to reach the clouds and the clouds wandered around in the blue sky. Rivers started to flow and trees started to get a greenish image. Birds started to sing; so did Robin with the red hat.

Robin, with the red hat, lived in the trees day and night waiting for the spring. Today was a beautiful day so Robin decided to fly around with his red hat on his head.

Robin looked up at the shining sun. He looked down at the river. He looked right toward the trees and then looked left toward the big city.

Robin started to fly toward the city. When he reached it, he sat on the roof of a house. He felt hungry.

"I must have something to eat," he said to himself.

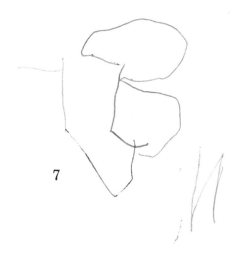

Robin went inside the house and looked at the wall. There he saw another big robin with a red hat the same as his. That robin was in a big mirror on the wall. Robin then went into the kitchen.

Robin sat on the cookie jar and ate five cookies. Now Robin was very thirsty.

Robin saw a jug with a little water in it. He reached for the water but his red hat dropped right into the water.

Robin tried to get his hat out of the jug, but his beak didn't reach to the water.

Suddenly a door opened and a little girl came into the kitchen carrying a bucket of water. She saw Robin sitting at the edge of the jug, trying to reach the red hat.

"Oh, there is a little Robin with a red hat. I'll help you, little red-hatted Robin."

The little girl started to pour the water from her bucket into the jug. As the little girl put in more water, Robin watched his red hat slowly come closer and closer to the top of the jug. The jug became full of water. The little girl picked the red hat out of the jug and put it back on Robin's head.

Robin gave her a big smile and flew away.